Love Puppies

WE'RE HERE TO HELP!

Recipe for Success

JaNay Brown-Wood

SCHOLASTIC INC.

*To my Aunt Netty, whose superb baking skills
inspired me to keep baking new things,
even when it was tough!*

ISBN 978-1-338-83412-3

10 9 8 7 6 5 4 3 2 1   23 24 25 26 27

Printed in the U.S.A.   40

First printing 2023

Book design by Omou Barry

Decorative design border art © Shutterstock.com

Fall in love with each paw-fectly sweet adventure!

TABLE OF CONTENTS

Chapter 1
A Dinner Unserved

"Nachos, nachos, yeaaaaah," sang Clyde as he flew

through the air with a pair of tongs in paw. "I'm

gonna eat some nachos, yeah."

Clyde hovered over a small grill where thin slices

of steak sizzled and steamed. He took a sniff. The

aroma of spices and meat made his tummy growl and his tail dance. "I said nachos, nachos, yeah," he continued, flipping the steaks with his tongs.

This new recipe was one he had worked on for quite some time but never got right.

Seasonings too bland or too spicy.

Meat overcooked or not done enough.

Too much cheese.

Not enough veggies.

Zero bone bits.

But Clyde was *sure* this time would be just right.

Or at least, he hoped.

"Dinnertiiiiiiime," Clyde called to his Love Puppy pals after placing the steak slices onto each plate of nachos. He topped the dishes off with a sprinkle of bone bits.

"Smells pup-tastic," said Noodles the labradoodle. Her glowing nose led the way into the kitchen, and the smile on her puppy face shone as bright as a glistening rainbow.

Noodles was magical—all the pups were. Noodles could control the elements of weather to help the Love Puppies when they needed. Also, her nose could tell when others were feeling strong emotions, like the excitement Clyde was feeling right at that moment.

"Can't wait to dig in!" said Noodles. She climbed onto a chair at the dinner table.

"Neither can I," said Barkley, a tiny dachshund who magically appeared in the chair beside Noodles.

"Oh!" yipped Clyde and Noodles, startled by Barkley's sudden appearance.

"That never gets old," giggled Barkley. He had always had the ability to morph into *anything*, but a recent mission had taught Barkley that he could disappear and even camouflage, too! Barkley's powers definitely came in handy when the pups were out on one of their missions.

Noodles sent a warm wind Barkley's way, ruffling his ears as the three pups laughed.

Just then, Rosie bounded into the room with a bouquet of roses between her teeth. She hurried over to an empty vase that sat on the countertop and gently placed the flowers into it. Next, she carefully carried the vase to the dining room table. With a swish of her nose, the flowers shimmered and grew two sizes bigger.

"There," she said. The bouquet made the dinner table look excellent. That was Rosie's power: flower magic. As the leader of the puppy team, her ability to control plants and flowers never ceased to amaze. "Roses are the perfect touch for a fancy dinner table."

"You mean the *paw*-fect touch," said Barkley.

"Of course," said Rosie, tickling Barkley's chin as she passed him and made her way to her own seat.

"Welcome to your dinner," said Clyde, flying belly-up while balancing all four plates on his upturned paws. Clyde's power was flight. He could soar through the air with ease anytime he pleased!

As Clyde stopped at the table, Noodles helped by sending airstreams that lifted the plates and set them down in front of each puppy.

Clyde took his place next to Noodles and Rosie. "Okay, Pups," he called, "dinner is served. I call this 'Na-cho Grandpup's Nachos,'" he said with a chuckle. "*Bone* appétit."

Just as each pup opened their mouths to take giant bites, flashing lights stopped them cold. Noodles's nose lit up like a birthday cake, as did the bright heart on Rosie's chest. Barkley's body flashed in and out of view, and a buzz filled the dining room as the Crystal Bone made its appearance, levitating through the kitchen toward the table. It vibrated and flashed—pink, purple, orange, and blue.

"Uh-oh," said Rosie with worry on her puppy face.

But all the pups knew what this meant: A new mission was waiting for them.

"But . . . but—" began Clyde.

"I know, Clydie," said Rosie in a gentle tone. "You worked so hard on this. But dinner will have to wait. Somebody, somewhere, needs our help. Let's go, Pups."

Off dashed Rosie, Noodles, and Barkley, following the Crystal Bone. It led the way toward the living room of the Love Puppy Headquarters, also known as the Doghouse.

Clyde stayed back. He hurried over to the kitchen cabinets and pulled out four large bowls. He placed each bowl down over the plates of nachos. "Hopefully, this will keep them warm enough," he said to himself, "for when we eat them in just a minute."

But he knew. With a new mission, it would keep the pups busy for hours.

My Na-cho Grandpup's Nachos would be nach-so good *if they were cold and soggy,* he thought to himself.

That would be okay, though, if it meant the team would help someone in need.

When a mission called, hungry tummies had to wait.

And with how quickly the Bone alerted the pups, Clyde could tell this mission was going to be a doozy.

Chapter 2
Two Boys and a Bakeoff

When Clyde entered the room, everyone was already in place.

"There you are, Pup!" said Rosie who stood on her hind legs with her paws hovering over the Crystal Bone, ready to receive a message.

The Crystal Bone wasn't just a regular bone the pups chewed on or played with. It was a crystalline message center that sent missions to Rosie, the Love Puppy leader. Rosie's paw pads glowed bright pink. She gently placed them onto the slick surface of the Bone and closed her eyes.

"Oh," she said. "Hmmmm, very interesting."

"What is it?" asked Barkley. Each of the pups sat on the carpet on all sides of the Bone, watching Rosie with tails waggling fiercely. "What did the Bone say?"

After a moment more, Rosie said, "Show them please, Bone." She pulled her paws from the Bone and sat on all fours. A vivid light flashed from the Bone. Right at the Bone's surface, a hologram image of a young boy emerged. Then the rest of the scene appeared.

The boy stood in a kitchen beside a woman who was stirring a large bowl with a wooden spoon. She handed him the bowl and the two of them mixed together, him holding the bowl, her stirring with the spoon. They smiled and laughed. The two continued on, mixing and placing things into pans and then into the oven.

Suddenly, the Bone changed the hologram scene, and this time, the boy walked into a crowded room handing out the treats he and the woman had just made. People patted him on the back, complimenting him on the dish. Even though it was only a hologram, the boy's happiness shined through like starlight.

"Sho' tastes good, son," said a voice.

"You made this?" asked another.

"Jayden, you are so talented," said another voice.

"Well, I helped Auntie," the boy answered. "We made it together."

The Bone switched up the scene one last time. This time, the boy stood in a kitchen by himself. He mixed something in a bowl then stopped. He dipped his finger in for a taste. He coughed and slammed the bowl down and charged from the room. The hologram burned out.

"This is Jayden," said Rosie as the Bone projected words onto the ceiling, "and he's our next mission."

> **NAME: JAYDEN WRIGHT**
> **Age:** 8
> **Grade:** Just finished third grade but is off for the summer
> **Problem:** Wants to enter the Young Baker Summer Bakeoff

"A bakeoff!" said Clyde, his body lifting from the ground like his excitement was helium gas, filling him like a balloon. "That sounds PUP-TASTIC!" Clyde shot through the air and cartwheeled along the ceiling. There he flipped, right in front of the animated banner pups who yipped and jumped in their fabric flags that hung along the walls.

"This is definitely your speed, Clydie," said Rosie. She and the others laughed at Clyde's in-air antics.

"Well, what are we waiting for? Let's go investigate," called Clyde.

All the pups put their paws in the center of a huddle. Their paw pads glowed—Rosie's pink, Noodles's orange, Barkley's purple, and Clyde's— who swooped down just in time—bright blue.

"With the power of love, anything is possible! Love Puppies, go!"

* * *

The puppies landed on top of bleachers next to a football field. There was a school building and a parking lot nearby. The pups looked around for a second, confused. Where was Jayden? Usually, the Doggie Door—the Love Puppy Portal—placed the pups exactly where they needed to be for any mission they were on. It was odd that it landed them in this particular spot.

Just then, the pups could hear voices coming from beside the bleachers.

"I know, man," said a boy's voice. "I can't believe Summerland is doing it, too! A bakeoff?!"

Barkley's head disappeared into thin air as he leaned over the side of the bleachers and looked down to see where the voices were coming from. "It's him!" he said, sitting back up straight. "It's Jayden! And somebody else."

"It sounds awesome," said another voice. "What was the prize again, Jay?"

"I don't remember. Let me see." Jayden's voice got closer to the pups, and suddenly, he was standing right next to them, pulling a crinkled piece of paper from his pocket.

"'Young Baker Summer Bakeoff. A competition just for kids!'" read Jayden. "Adults can only help with tricky stuff like using knives and ovens, but everything else is made by kid bakers. Then it says . . . 'Kid bakers who enter cannot use recipes but must make up their own.'"

Jayden stopped and gulped. "Our own recipes? That's gonna be hard, DeAndre."

"What? That ain't stopped us before," said DeAndre. "Remember when we made that lemon pudding stuff without a recipe? It was good."

"Yeah, it was all right," said Jayden.

"Well, read the rest of the flyer, Jay. You haven't even said the prize yet."

Jayden lifted the paper again. "'Each baker must make two different treats from scratch with their own recipes. One must be a cookie and the other can be a treat of the baker's choosing. Then the bakers will have to make one more mystery recipe given to them by the judges. Everything will be judged on Taste, Presentation, and Creativity.'"

"What's the prize?! What's the prize?!" interrupted DeAndre.

"Oh yeah. Third place is a hundred and fifty dollars and a trophy. Second place—"

"We don't care about those. What's the grand prize?"

"Dre, it's FIVE HUNDRED DOLLARS!"

"Five hundred dollars! What?!" Both boys jumped up and down and cheered.

"We'd be almost rich!" laughed Jayden as they high-fived each other. "I could buy so much."

"That's like ten video games," said Dre.

"Or a new skateboard," said Jayden.

At that, a loud whoosh sounded off nearby. Both

DeAndre and Jayden snapped their heads in the direction of the noise.

"The bus!" called the boys, and they dashed out the gate toward the giant bus that was nearing their pickup stop.

"They're not going to make it," called Rosie.

"Not if I can help it!" said Noodles. She kicked up a wind that pushed the boys from behind and launched them toward the bus's door. Just as the door began to close, the boys landed on the bus steps.

"Get on in here," said the bus driver. The doors closed, and the bus pulled away with Jayden and DeAndre inside.

"That was close. Good thinking, Noodles!" said Rosie.

"Did you see how excited they got about the prize?" said Clyde. "They both really want to win."

"I think Jayden's got the stuff," said Rosie. "And with a little Pup Power, I have a feeling we'll have a win on our paws."

"This mission should be a piece of cake," giggled Clyde. "Let's follow that bus to Jayden's to get all the clues we need to seal this deal."

Barkley morphed into a hoverboard, and Rosie and Noodles hopped on, with Clyde flying beside them.

"Love Puppies," said Rosie, "let's GO!"

Chapter 3
Planning for a Win?

"Auntie!" called Jayden as he and DeAndre burst through the door of a first-floor apartment. The Love Puppies positioned themselves by a window that overlooked the kitchen, which was hidden behind a bush. No one could see them from the street.

"Hey, Auntie!" Jayden called again, his voice echoing from down the hallway.

The pups watched as a tall woman with dark skin moved around the kitchen. She wore an apron and had smudges of flour on her young-looking face.

"In here, boys," she called. Jayden and DeAndre bounded into the kitchen.

"Auntie, guess what—" started Jayden.

"Ah-ah," said Auntie, stopping him with a smile. "Sugar first. Story next."

Jayden laughed and kissed her on the cheek. "Hi, Auntie," he said.

"Hi, Jay. Uh, you too, young man," she said, eyeing DeAndre.

"Hi, Ms. Kreisha," he said, also kissing her on the cheek.

"Hi, Dre," she said back with a smile. "Okay. Now, what's all this excitement about?"

"Auntie, guess what? Summerland camp is having a bakeoff!" Jayden said.

Both boys went back and forth, explaining the rules to Auntie. When they told her what the prize for first place was, they started jumping up and down, dancing, and high-fiving each other.

"Five hundred dollars? Wow!" said Auntie, their joy and excitement wrapping around her.

Noodles's nose was in full-blast mode, bathing the puppies in orange light. "So much happiness coming from that little kitchen," she whispered as the pups continued watching.

"Isn't it wonderful?" said Rosie. Behind them, the bush began sprouting bright pink roses that danced in Noodles's slight breeze.

After the boys stopped jumping and celebrating, they calmed themselves, sitting at a table and watching Auntie pull something from the oven.

"Jay, grab the peaches, please," she said.

He jumped up and grabbed a bowl of strained peaches from the counter. Then he pulled out a knife and cutting board and began slicing the pieces.

"Remember your fingers," Auntie said, watching Jayden with the knife. "Slow and steady." She plated her treat and added Jayden's peaches and a dallop of whipped cream.

The smell was amazing. Like peaches dancing with gingerbread and brown sugar and butter. And Clyde could tell it tasted wonderful, too, by how the boys smacked their lips and said "mmm" over and over again. Also, by how the treat only lasted on their plates for about a minute and a half until it was inhaled.

This got Clyde's tummy grumbling again. His mind went back to the plates of untouched nachos that the pups had left behind.

"Five hundred dollars, Auntie," said Jayden after finishing his last bite.

"Yeah, but we have to make it past the first round, though," said DeAndre, having finished his plate, too. "Our camp counselor said judges at our summer camp are gonna pick the finalists next Friday."

"And the final bakeoff is at the convention center. Could you imagine how happy everybody would be if I won the whole thing? Like Granddad and all the aunties and uncles and everybody."

"Yeah, they'd be happy," said Auntie. "They would be very proud. Honestly, they'd be just as proud if you gave it your best."

Jayden rolled his eyes and DeAndre chuckled a little.

"Well, we like winning," DeAndre said.

"Then, what's your plan?" she asked.

The boys stared at each other in silence. DeAndre shrugged his shoulders and Jayden said: "To win?"

"I see," said Auntie. "It's best if you each make a plan of action. Plan out *how* you are going to win. Which recipes are you going to build off of? What tweaks are you going to make? You know, strategize."

The boys nodded their heads as they cleared their plates.

"I'll think about a plan when I get home," said DeAndre, pulling his backpack onto his back. Strategizing did sound like a good idea. "See you later, Jay," he said, quickly doing their handshake. "Let's get that win!"

The pups looked at one another. Inside Clyde's tummy swirled a whole bunch of feelings. And a whole bunch of questions swirled around in his head.

If Jayden's auntie was already an excellent baker and had good ideas about making plans, why did Jayden need the puppies at all?

Chapter 4
Less than Egg-cellent

The puppy's concern about whether they were needed or not only grew as they continued to watch Jay and his auntie in the kitchen.

"All right now, Jay," his auntie said, "I want to try out this new recipe I've been working on. I need you to whisk nine egg whites." Auntie held a bright pink piece of paper that she had written on. She read it over as Jayden walked to the refrigerator, a little less pep in his step than the pups had seen earlier.

Noodles's nose began to blink—some kind of emotion was building in the room.

"What is it, pretty pup?" asked Rosie.

"Not sure yet," answered Noodles.

Jay carried a carton of eggs to the countertop along with a large glass bowl. He positioned an egg over the side of the bowl and took a deep breath.

"You sure you want *me* to do the egg whites?" he finally asked, looking up at Auntie.

"Yes, I do," she said. She wrote down a few more notes onto her bright pink recipe page.

"You know I'm no good at egg whites," he reminded her.

Noodles's nose grew a bit brighter as they watched.

"Jay, you are good at so many things. Like singing at church, and your violin. And your football team?"

Jay blushed. "Yeah, I'm pretty good at those things. But they all come easy. I don't even have to think about them. It's like I was just *born* good at those things."

"Still took practice, right? Practice singing. Practice playing? Drill after drill on the field?"

"I guess," he said. "But baking is different. I'm

only good at it when I'm helping you. Dre is good at it all the time."

"Pssshh," said Auntie. "You are just as good as Dre. And what'll be even better about this competition is that you guys get to do it together."

Jayden frowned, but his eyes met Auntie's.

"Plus," she continued "you are helping me right now, aren't you? So, stop dragging your feet and get back to cracking those eggs." She chuckled.

Jayden took another deep breath and carefully tapped the egg. He poured the wet egg into his cupped hand, letting some of the clear liquid drop into the bowl.

Noodles's nose flickered some more.

Next, Jay dropped the shell back into the carton, and then tipped the content of the egg from one of his cupped hands, to the other, letting more clear liquid drip into the bowl. He did this a few times until only the egg yolk remained in his hand. He smiled and disposed of the yolk.

"See? One down, eight more to go," said Auntie.

Jayden repeated this two, three, four more times, and Auntie eyed him quietly as she worked on a different part of the recipe.

"Pups," said Barkley while Jayden cracked egg number five, "I'm still not seeing what Jayden needs from us. He seems to be pretty good in the kitchen."

Clyde nodded. Separating egg whites was no easy thing to do!

"Yeah," said Rosie, "I'm not either. And all this good-smelling food has me pretty hungry. I believe we have a delicious dinner waiting for us at home, right, Clydie? Are we ready to call it a day and head back to plan out our next move?"

"Sounds good to me," said Clyde. He still wasn't sure what he'd do about *his* dish of now too-cold, too-mushy, no-longer-fresh Na-cho Grandpup's Nachos. But he felt pretty confident he'd think of something.

"Well then, let's go," said Rosie.

But right at that very moment, "AW MAN!" filled the kitchen.

The pups looked over at Jayden. A line of milky, yellow yolk stretched from one of his hands to the other, with most of it landing right in the glass bowl.

Clyde sucked in a huge breath, filling his little pup lungs all the way up. How was Jayden going to fix *that*?

"I messed it up! I told you, Auntie!" yelled Jayden. "I messed up your whole recipe! You shouldn't have let me do the dumb egg whites! I'm the worst at this!"

"Now, hold on," Auntie said in a gentle, soft voice. "We have more eggs. You can do it again."

But Jayden could barely hear her. He turned on the tap, washed his hands, and placed the ruined egg whites into the empty sink. He kept his eyes on the floor and wouldn't look up at Auntie, even when she reminded him that he could try again.

Just before he stormed out of the kitchen, he turned, eyes still glued to the floor, and said, "I can bake with you, Auntie, but not by myself. I'm the worst at making stuff by myself. So, I'm not doing the competition. I'm dropping out!"

"Jay Baby," she said softly.

But he had already left the room.

The pups watched this while holding their breath. Clyde's tummy rumbled some more, but it was more like it was all tied up in knots inside instead of hungry.

"Why did Jayden just give up like that? Everybody makes mistakes," he said to the pups as Auntie pulled out a fresh carton of eggs and began separating the egg whites with ease.

The bigger problem, though, was if the whole mission was to help Jayden compete in the bakeoff, how could they do that if he'd already decided to drop out?

What would the pups do if their mission was over before it even began?

Chapter 5
Third Time's the Charm

By now, the pups were pressed against the window looking as far into the apartment as they could. Jayden was out of sight, in a back room somewhere. But Auntie continued working on her new recipe.

"Are we sure that the Crystal Bone said we're

supposed to help him win the bakeoff?" Clyde asked the other pups.

"Maybe not win, but at least make it past the camp bakeoff to the finals," said Rosie.

"Jayden Baby!" called Auntie again. She was whipping up the egg whites in her bowl. With the sixth egg, she, too, dropped a glob of egg yolk in on accident. "Whoops—" she said. "Jayden, come on back out here, please. I want to show you something."

"How are we supposed to make him stay in the competition?" asked Barkley.

The twisty-turvy feeling came back to Clyde's tummy. Jayden still hadn't come out and Clyde wasn't sure how to answer Barkley's question.

Could *Clyde* teach Jayden how to separate egg whites? He could do that in his sleep—well, after many, many tries and fails.

But just because Clyde knew how to do it didn't mean he knew how to teach Jayden how to do it. And how could he teach Jayden without being seen? None of these ideas seemed like good ones.

Suddenly, Clyde had the urge to whip up some egg whites himself, just to check to make sure he could—and to ease some of the worry he felt swimming around inside him.

"How do we help him?" Clyde asked, covering his face with his paws. His tail wagged wildly, and his stomach somersaulted behind his belly button. "How do we help him?" he asked again.

"Deep breaths, Pup," said Rosie. She patted him softly. "We'll figure something out."

"There you are," said Auntie gently.

Each pup looked up from Clyde and back into the kitchen. Jayden stood in the doorway. His shoulders slouched and he still looked everywhere but at Auntie.

"Come here. I want to show you something." She leaned her egg white bowl over. "See? No big deal. You just start over. I'll put these aside for a different recipe that calls for egg yolks. Want to help me a third time?"

Jayden shrugged his shoulders.

Auntie separated the eggs, one by one, until there were only three left.

"Go wash your hands, Jay. My hands are getting tired. Finish off these for me, please," she said with a smile on her face.

"But—"

"No buts," she interjected.

Jayden followed directions. He joined her in front of the bowl and breathed deeply.

First egg—separated perfectly. He dropped the shells into the carton.

Second egg—another perfect separation.

"Last one," said Auntie.

"I really think you should do it," he said.

Auntie rubbed her wrists and twisted them like she was trying to relieve pressure.

Jayden took another breath. He steadied his hands. Last egg—

"He did it," whispered Clyde. All the eggs had been separated, and Jayden went on to whip them up into what Auntie called "stiff peaks."

"What I tell you?" said Auntie. "Nothing that a second or third try can't perfect." She and Jayden cleaned up the rest of the kitchen after removing the dessert with freshly made meringue from the oven. "Let it sit for just a moment more," she said, patting Jayden on the shoulder as he sat at the table, "then feel free to taste it."

"Okay, Auntie."

"And, you know, Jayden Baby, I really hope you try to do the bakeoff. Just to challenge yourself to do something new. Something that you have to work at to improve."

"I'll think about it," he said.

"But we'll be proud of you, anyway, no matter what you choose. No matter what you do. Good night, baby."

"Good night."

Jayden stood and walked over to the refrigerator where he had hung the bakeoff flyer with a magnet.

"Okay," Jayden whispered to himself, just barely loud enough for the puppies to hear. "I'll give the bakeoff a try. For Auntie." With that, he turned the light off and left the kitchen.

And just as quickly as it had seemed over, the pups were back on track to accomplish another mission.

"There's still hope for Jayden," said Rosie as a giant yawn escaped her. "We need a brainstorming session ASAP. But it'll have to wait until the morning," she said, looking at the stars shining above.

Even though they'd spent the whole evening learning about Jayden, they were still at a loss for what to do.

"Let's head home, Pups. Our doggie beds await," said Rosie.

But Clyde's tummy got to twisting again. How could they all sleep with no idea of how to help?

Chapter 6
Sugar, Spice, and
Clydie—So Nice!

Clyde tossed and turned through the night.

He kept picturing Jayden upset after ruining his

auntie's dish. Clyde thought about how quickly

Jayden gave up and how he said he liked to do things that came easy to him.

But baking didn't come easy—not for most people *or* pups. It came from practice and failure and practice some more. And finally, getting it right.

So how could you help someone who didn't want to fail?

All these questions kept Clyde wide-awake.

Just as the sun began rising, an idea jumped into his head. It sent him sailing over to his desk for some paper and a pen.

Clyde wrote something down. He wrote some more and then stopped and looked it over. Then he scratched out some of his words and added other words.

He held the sheet of paper up to the sunlight.

Clyde made a beeline for the kitchen and got right to work. He pulled mixing bowls from cabinets and spoons from drawers. He grabbed ingredients from the refrigerator and snipped some herbs from Rosie's windowsill herb garden.

He zipped and zoomed through the kitchen stirring and swishing, measuring and mixing, placing and plating, too.

"Clydie," said a groggy voice coming from the hallway. "Is that you, Pup?" Rosie shuffled from around the corner, wiping her eyes. Right behind her came Noodles with her nightcap still in place—the giant pom pom flopped right in front of her

49

face. Behind her slumped Barkley who yawned such a big yawn that he went tumbling into Noodles. *FLOP!*

"That's better," he said, now lying down on her soft fur.

"Get up, silly pup," said Rosie, "we've got to check in on Clydie." She turned her face toward Clyde. "Are you okay, Pup? It's five o'clock in the morning."

"Oh, I'm doing pup-tastic," he said, his voice sounding as excited as a human child on their birthday. "I got this idea for a new recipe, and I *had* to try it out!" He flew back over to the refrigerator and began digging through it.

Rosie looked around at the kitchen—Clyde had

whipped up quite a mess. Eggshells, white puddles, and spice spills all along the countertops mingled with used bowls, spoons, and whisks.

But the air smelled amazing. Like cinnamon and other yummy fragrances that the other pups could not figure out. Whatever it was, it made their tummies grumble with delight.

"It's almost ready," said Clyde, coming back to the counter with a container of fancy-looking bacon.

"So how are we going to help Jayden out?" barked Barkley as he and the other pups sat on the stools at the countertop, still watching Clyde cook.

"That's a good question, Barkley Boy," said Rosie. "This is Clydie's domain."

"Yeah, Clyde, you are great at making tasty treats. What do *you* think we should do to help?"

But Clyde didn't answer. It was clear he was in his zone. He stirred something that bubbled in a pot. Next, he chopped up some bacon and dropped it into a sizzling pan.

"I just need to make the sauce!" Clyde said. He zoomed back to the refrigerator and cabinets, pulling out containers of berries, sugar, and some other things. He tossed the ingredients into another heated pot and began squishing and stirring them up.

"Clydie," Rosie said, finally making eye contact with him, "how do you make food so yummy?"

"I don't know," Clyde said as he picked up a

few spices and began tipping them into the pot. "I just—OOOPS!"

The pups sucked in a breath as Clyde peered into his pot. He carefully dipped one puppy-paw claw and brought it to his lips.

"WOOF!" he cried. "So much for that batch. Put the temperature on too high. On to try two," he said, pulling out the same ingredients as before and adding them to the freshly rinsed pot.

"You're starting over, just like Jayden's auntie did," said Barkley.

"Sometimes you have to," said Clyde.

"But how do you know what ingredients to put in? You don't have a recipe," said Rosie.

"I used to use recipes when I was just starting out." Clyde tipped in a few more spices, then took another taste and smacked his lips. "But after practicing with them for so long, I didn't need them anymore. Now I just write my own!"

He zipped back over to the cabinet and grabbed a lemon. "Almost there," he said, slicing the lemon in half. "This just needs a little bit of . . ." Carefully, he squeezed the lemon into the simmering pan. "Pawfect! It's ready! Plate me please, Noodles."

Noodles used her wind to open the cabinets and pull out plates. Clyde slid on oven mitts and grabbed a baking sheet from the oven. It was lined with browned, bone-shaped biscuits of some sort.

He used a spatula to pull up the biscuits, placing one on each plate. Then he split each one in half.

On one half of each bone biscuit, he spooned some of the bacon syrup he had stirred up earlier. On the other half, he spooned on some of the berry sauce. Clyde pushed the plates in front of each pup.

"This is sooooooo gooooooood," howled Barkley before diving back into his plate. The pups lapped it up until their plates were spotless and their tummies were full.

"Incredible, Clydie," said Rosie with a huge smile on her face.

"So, is that how you make food so yummy?" said Noodles. "Just by doing it?"

"Practice, I guess," said Clyde, who now sat calmly in a chair next to Rosie. "Maybe if I just keep trying, I'll figure it out."

"And you didn't care about making a mistake," said Barkley. "You added something else and tried something new."

Clyde nodded his head. "I guess so."

"But I remember it wasn't always that way," added Noodles. "Remember when you made the apple-flavored bone bites."

"Double woof," laughed Clyde.

"That was an epic fail," said Noodles. "But you kept trying, and that's how you came up with that apple kibble crunch! That's still my favorite Clyde dish."

Clyde smiled, his cheeks blushing slightly. "You can't be scared to try something new, even if you might fail at it. It's the messing up that makes you get better. At least, that's how it is for me when I make stuff."

"Clydie, those are great ideas of what to do! I'm sure an idea like this could definitely help Jayden. What was his first bakeoff task again?"

"Cookies," said Clyde.

"What should we do to help him first?" asked Rosie.

An idea flashed across Clyde's face. With a flick of his tail and a flying flip, Clyde knew just what to do! "Follow me, Pups!"

Chapter 7
A Not-So-Sweet Treat

The puppies dashed after Clyde. He flew out of the kitchen, down the hallway, and into his bedroom. All along his walls were posters of different foods like filet mignon, beef Wellington, and cookie crunch parfaits. He also had corkboards filled with written-out recipes pinned to them.

Clyde jetted to a large bookshelf that sat next to his window. He flew to the top, looking over the books. "'Chicken recipes, veggie dishes, scrumptious soups,'" he read aloud, moving from spine to spine. "'Cakes, pies, pastries'—aha! Here they are!"

Clyde pulled out a stack of books and floated down to the ground where the other pups waited eagerly.

"And here it is," he said, showing them the book on top.

"A cookie cookbook?" said Barkley.

"Yes! This is the first cookie cookbook that I used to learn how to make cookies. And these are the other ones. They all helped me practice."

"Jayden can't use other recipes, remember? He has to come up with his own," said Noodles.

"That's true," said Clyde, "but this is how I got good at making cookies. I used these all the time. They helped me know just what to put into a cookie to make it *really* tasty."

"So then, what's the plan, Clydie?" asked Rosie.

"I'll let him borrow these so he can get some practice making delicious cookies. It's got to work! I know because it worked for me!"

"Paws in, Pups!" said Rosie. "We've got a young baker to visit!"

WHOOSH!

It was still pretty early when the pups landed

outside Jayden's kitchen. They hurried back to their window-side waiting spot.

"Look, the window is cracked just enough," whispered Barkley. While it was open slightly, it was too small for the pups to slide their paws in to open it wider.

"I've got it," said Barkley. His body started to morph from Puppy-Barkley to Balloon-Barkley!

"Slide me right there," he said with a high-pitched voice.

"You sound so funny, Barkley!" giggled Noodles. She slipped the purple Balloon-Barkley in between the window and the window frame.

Barkley began filling with air—little by

little—pushing the window open more and more. When it was open wide enough, the team of magical pups pushed through to deliver the cookbooks.

Barkley morphed back into his puppy body. Working together and quickly, the pups climbed inside and placed the books on the kitchen table.

Finally, Barkley changed into a pen and wrote a short note that he left beside the books.

"He'll think Auntie got these for him—for sure!" whispered Barkley.

"Good work, Pups. Let's get out of here," directed Rosie.

As Barkley began sliding the window closed, once all four pups were safely back outside, the kitchen light clicked on. Jayden staggered in, yawning and stretching. He walked over to the refrigerator and stared at it for a moment, his eyes reading the flyer again.

He sighed and looked over to the table.

"What the—" He hurried over to the stack of books and lifted the note. "'To Jay. Just for practice.' Wow!" he said.

Jayden sat down and began flipping through the books, one after the next. "So many good ones. Which should I try first?" he said to himself, using his finger to run it down the page. "Oooh, double chocolate chunk sounds great!"

Jayden jumped up, washed his hands, and began

collecting the ingredients and bowls and spoons. One canister after another, Jayden carried the items to the table.

"He's so excited," said Noodles, her nose glowing through the window.

"This was an A-plus plan, Clydie," said Rosie.

Jayden rubbed his hands together and began. "'One cup softened butter.'" He grabbed two sticks of butter and put them a microwave-safe bowl. "Twenty seconds should do it," he said pushing the buttons and starting the microwave.

"Okay, powdered sugar next." Jayden reached for one of the unmarked canisters of white powder. The microwave beeping stopped him. "Butter's ready."

He slipped the softened butter into the bowl.

"So far, so good," said Barkley.

But Clyde watched closely. His tummy began twisting again. Something seemed off.

"'Two cups of powdered sugar.' Got it!" said Jayden, scooping up two cups from the canister and plopping them into the bowl. A little white cloud puffed up from the bowl.

"Oh no!" said Clyde, sitting up straight. "That's not powdered sugar—that's flour!"

The pups looked on with concern as Jayden made mistake after mistake. Each time, Clyde called out in horror saying things like:

"—that's not enough vanilla!" or "That says four

hundred and fifty degrees—that's too high for cookies!"

By the time Jayden was ready to put them in the oven, Clyde hid his face in his paws while his stomach somersaulted like an energetic gymnast.

Jayden raced out of the room and then back in, followed by an older boy.

"Durrell, can you put those in the oven for me? Auntie said I can't use the oven by myself yet."

The older boy shrugged and put the cookies in. Shortly after, the same boy returned to pull them out after the timer went off.

"These look kinda dark," said Durrell, placing the sheet on the stovetop.

"They're supposed to look like that," said Jayden.

"Okay," said Durrell, grabbing a napkin and one of the fresh cookies and walking out of the kitchen just as Auntie walked in.

"Morning, babies," said Auntie, all dressed up for work. "Cookies in the morning," she said to Jayden, giving him a kiss on the forehead. "Don't mind if I do!"

"I'll get the milk," he said, bouncing over to the refrigerator and cabinet. "They're called double chocolate chunk."

"They sure smell good," she said.

Jayden and Auntie both grabbed up a cookie.

"On three, okay—one, two, three!"

Both took a bite. Jayden gagged and Auntie chewed stiffly with a smile on her face.

"I can taste the chocolate," she said with her mouth still filled with cookie.

"See, what did I tell you?" Jayden said, dropping his cookie and folding his arms across his chest. "I'm no baker like you, Auntie. I stink at this and I'm going to embarrass myself in that stupid competition."

"Mistakes happen. It's a part of the learning."

"I'm going back to bed," said Jayden in a quiet voice. "Have a good day at work, Auntie."

Noodles's nose burned brightly.

That was a Great Dane–sized failure. Was Jayden going to drop out again—but this time for good?

Chapter 8
Practice Makes Paw-fect

By midday, Jayden still hadn't come back into the kitchen. Not even to finish cleaning it up.

"We should probably head home, give him time to burn off some steam," said Rosie. "It was still a great plan, though."

But Clyde felt heavy with disappointment. He didn't want to just leave Jayden feeling so down. Yet, he put his paw in the middle of their circle and followed the pups back through the Doggie Door portal.

The pups headed into their rooms to think, but Clyde returned to the kitchen.

How had that gone so doggone bad? he thought to himself. The cookbooks had been great at helping him learn. But what went wrong?

Clyde pulled out all the ingredients for the double chocolate chunk cookies—he'd memorized almost all the recipes in those books. But instead of chocolate, he placed bacon chunks onto the cutting board. No chocolate for dogs, even magical puppies.

Clyde began adding in ingredients. He dumped in powdered sugar.

"See, Jayden, it's sugar. *Not* flour," Clyde said to himself. But, he had to admit, powdered sugar did kind of look like flour, to an untrained eye at least.

Clyde moved on to the eggs. "Here's how you crack an egg without dropping in the shell, Jayden. It just takes practice," Clyde said aloud. Pretending to teach Jayden was at least helping soothe his twisty-turvy tummy a little bit.

By the time Clyde finished the cookies, cleaned the kitchen, and jotted down some more ideas for recipes to try, the rest of the pups trotted in. Clyde slumped on the countertop next to the cookies, chin in his paws.

"Smells delicious in here," said Barkley. "But it always does after a Clyde-Cooking session."

Clyde pushed the plate of double bacon chunk cookies, but he still didn't lift his head.

Rosie patted his face. "Did making the cookies help you feel better?" she asked.

Just then, Noodles and Barkley began howling in delight after biting into the warm treats.

"Soooooo gooooood!" they howled, their tails wagging a hundred miles a minute.

Rosie joined in after tasting the cookies, too.

"Thanks, guys," said Clyde. But it didn't help

him to feel better. Clearly, Clyde being an excellent baker wasn't going to help Jayden become one, too.

"You know," said Barkley after his fourth cookie, "I'm starting to think that maybe Jayden *isn't* any good at baking. Because if treats are supposed to taste like this, his auntie's reaction says he is *far* from it."

Even though it was hard to swallow, Barkley had a point.

Clyde shook his head slowly. "But that's okay. That's how it is with everything. When you try it out for the first time, you stink at it!"

"These definitely don't stink!" said Rosie. She was working on her third cookie.

"Like you and your baking chops, Clyde—these cookies are perfect. Did you have to start over?" asked Noodles.

"No. But I've made them so many times before, I knew exactly what to do. I knew what flour looked like and how it wasn't powdered sugar. I just knew that stuff!"

"So not only did you have the practice, you had the right tools!" added Noodles. "I bet if you put in flour instead of sugar, your cookies would have been not-so-good, too."

After hearing Noodles's words, Clyde sat up straight. "You're right. The right tools!" Clyde said. "Practice with the right tools helps you get better. I know what to do next! We need Typewriter-Barkley and some labels. Let's get to it, Pups!"

Clyde typed sheet after sheet of labels on Typewriter-Barkley.

First thing in the morning, they'd help Jayden find his right tools!

"Puppy toes crossed this will work," said Clyde. He really hoped it would!

Chapter 9
A Dash of Magic and
a Peppermint Sprig

Early the next morning, the pups made their way

back to Jayden's home. Balloon-Barkley came in

handy again to open the window, and soon, all four

pups stood in Jayden's kitchen.

It was clean—all the countertops and the floors sparkled and shined.

Maybe Jayden had gone on a cleaning spree, too, just as Clyde had. Clyde began to realize that he really did have a lot in common with Jayden. Perhaps that was why Clydie's tummy got tied into knots at the thought of Jayden failing—it would mean that Clyde and the pups had failed, too.

But Clyde wasn't afraid of failure. He knew it helped him to grow.

"All right, Pups. Let's get to labeling," whispered Clyde. The Love Puppies swooped into action.

Sugar canister—check!

Flour, salt, spices, too—check!

Even measuring cups and spoons were labeled to make sure Jayden was using the correct ones. Then Clyde scooped up all the measuring cups and spoons, bowls, and other items that he knew would be helpful when preparing cookies. He laid them out on the round table in an organized way.

"Practice with the right tools," said Rosie with a wink. "I think we've done it, Pups!"

Rosie led the way back to the window. Up she went, with Clyde's help. Noodles blew a wind that elevated herself up and out the window. Next, it was Barkley's turn. But just as Barkley began to stretch his body like a firetruck ladder so he could grab onto the windowsill, Durrell walked in rubbing his eyes.

He stopped right in his tracks as he spotted four chubby pups huddled around the kitchen window.

"What the—" Durrell closed his eyes and rubbed them harder. This gave the pups a whole second to disappear from the window—but it was not enough time for Barkley to make it out.

But Barkley moved fast, flicking his tail and disappearing his body.

Durrell opened his eyes again and walked to the window, looking out. He looked to the left and right before shutting and locking it.

"I must be tripping," he said after he closed the window. "Better go back to bed before I start hallucinating again." Durrell flicked the light switch off and looked back at the window for a moment more. Nothing was there.

Then he shook his head and said, "Nah," and walked down the hall and out of sight.

"Come on, Pup," whispered Rosie who was no longer hiding beneath the window's flower basket. "Get out of there," she said, pressing her paws against the window.

"The window is locked," said Barkley, still invisible. "Hang on, I think I can open this," he said, stretching his invisible body so he could get right next to the latch.

"Wait, Barkley—here comes Jayden," called

Clyde. He was the first to spot Jayden coming down the hallway.

Jayden clicked the light on.

"I said I wasn't doing this anymore," Jayden said to no one. He slowly slumped over to the table and looked over the tools. He ran his finger over the labels. "Interesting," he said under his breath. He hopped up and hurried over to the cabinets.

"Wow! You didn't have to do this, Auntie," he said, looking at all the labels stuck on each jar. "Okay," he told himself. "I'll give it another try."

Jayden began a new recipe.

The pups watched as he turned on the oven and took a step toward the table.

"That's too high," Clyde whispered. "It should be three hundred and twenty-five degrees."

Jayden stopped. He scratched his head. He turned back to the oven and checked it—it did say 425. He looked around once again and turned the oven down to 325. "I gotta take my time and stop rushing through it," he said to himself.

"That was lucky," said Clyde. And that was true, too. If Jayden kept rushing through it, he'd mess up every time.

As Invisible-Barkley tried to sneakily crack open the window, Clyde watched Jayden make another mistake.

"Oh no!" called Clyde. "He grabbed a tablespoon,

not a teaspoon. Help him, Barkley, before it's too late!"

Jayden popped open a canister labeled SALT with the tablespoon in his hand.

"I can't look," said Rosie, hiding her face.

"Not on my watch," said Clyde. He took to the air and flew around the apartment building. The sound of a knock bounced off the wall of Jayden's apartment. Jayden hurried over and out of sight.

"Now, Barkley," called Clyde, who had zoomed back to the window. "Switch the spoons. He had a tablespoon. He needs a teaspoon."

Barkley kicked into action and swapped the spoons just in time.

"So weird," said Jayden to himself. "I *know* I heard someone at the door."

Jayden went back to work at the table, mixing in the correct amounts of the correct ingredients.

"This is looking way better!" said Noodles. Clyde nodded in agreement.

The pups continued to watch Jayden as Barkley tinkered with the window's lock. Then finally, *click* went the latch. Barkley squeezed a flattened paw between the window and wall and slid it open wide.

"Peppermint?" said Jayden. "Fresh peppermint. Do we even have that?" he said aloud. He walked over to the cabinet and looked inside.

"Uh-oh, this won't be good," said Clyde. Jayden

wasn't going to find fresh peppermint in the cabinet. Clyde and all the pups had gone through the cabinet when they were labeling—there was definitely no fresh peppermint.

"What about . . . 'sage'?" read Jayden, pulling the jar out.

"SAGE," cried Clyde. "That's a savory spice."

"Deep breaths, Clydie. I've got this," said Rosie. Then, right from the little bush that hid the pups from the street, grew one large sprig of fresh peppermint.

"Noodles, do your stuff," said Rosie as she plucked the sprig from the bush. Noodles sprinkled it with fresh raindrops to clean it, then kicked up a burst of wind that blew the peppermint sprig through the window and across the kitchen, where it landed right next to Jayden's bowl.

"Boy, it's breezy in here," he said. "Who opened that window?"

Right at that moment, Barkley shrank down to a bumblebee and buzzed out of the window and out of sight just as Jayden closed it tight.

The pups looked on as Jayden found the peppermint and smelled it. "Seems pepperminty to me," he said. He finished the recipe, and Durrell put the cookie sheets right into the oven.

At the beep of the timer, Durrell pulled them out. Both he and Jayden looked closely at them.

"Man, these smell ridiculous!" said

Durrell. "Let me get a taste of them."

Jayden used the spatula to scoop one off the sheet for Durrell and one for himself. Both boys blew on the hot cookies and took a bite.

"Jay—these are sick!" said Durrell. "You put yo' foot in these!" Durrell scooped up four more cookies onto a plate, poured a glass of milk, and left the kitchen.

Jayden lifted up some more cookies with his spatula and burst out of the apartment. He dashed across the street and banged on a door.

DeAndre appeared in the doorway.

"Whoa, what is going on, Jay?"

"You've got to try this. Taste this, Dre!" Jayden handed him a cookie.

"These are bomb," said Dre. "You made these? Man, these are winners!"

Jayden wore a smile as bright as all the sunrays mixed together.

"I think I'm getting the hang of this," he said to Dre. "Now I gotta just tweak the recipe and make it my own. I'm gonna try it again with my own ideas, you know? I'm gonna make them even better."

"You got this, Jay," said Dre. The two boys gave each other their signature handshake and said goodbye. Jayden strutted back over to his apartment.

"It's working," Clyde said. "It's finally working!"

The pups could tell it was only up from here!

Chapter 10
C is for Cookie . . . and Confidence

Except it wasn't up from here.

The pups looked over the kitchen after Jayden's second try: blackened cookies burnt to a crisp. It was a complete mess.

Jayden quickly cleaned up and then pulled out fresh ingredients to start a new batch of cookies. This time, he added everything slowly, with precision—no messed-up measurements, no too-fast stirring or overheated ovens.

A look of focus was on his face. He went through all the steps. Finally, Durrell put this new batch in and pulled them out when they were ready.

Jayden held a freshly baked cookie in his hand from a batch that he had played with and tweaked.

One he had made his own. A Jayden Original Recipe.

Jay took a bite.

Then he let out a deep sigh. He dropped the cookie and left the kitchen.

"Guess it didn't come out as he wanted," said Rosie.

"But he had really tried so hard this time," said Barkley.

That was clear. Jayden even took his time to make sure it was right.

"Failures are a part of the successes," reminded Clyde.

"Then how do we help him now?" asked Noodles.

"Well, when he did a good job, he really liked hearing how good everything tasted," said Clyde. "That makes *me* feel good, too."

"That's true," said Rosie. "We saw that in the Bone's

video and also when he made those yummy cookies."

"But he also seemed to like telling Auntie how tasty her creations were—that made him feel good, too," reminded Noodles. That was also true.

"And, he *loves* hanging out with DeAndre," added Clyde. "What if—Barkley, I'm going to need a letter."

Right there, outside the apartment window, the pups devised the next plan and typed it into action.

A little while later, a knock at the front door caused Jayden to emerge from his bedroom.

"Hello?" he said as he opened the door.

"Why'd you send me that note—oh man," said DeAndre after one look at his friend. "How bad is it, Jay?"

Jayden shrugged his shoulders.

DeAndre followed Jayden into the kitchen, carrying a plate of some cookies he had made. "Oh man!" he said again, running his eyes over the mess.

"I'm the worst at this, Dre. I don't even know why I'm trying. Every time I get in this dumb kitchen, I mess up!"

"Whoa, Jay. Take a breath, bro. It's all good. Don't worry about the mess-ups. They happen."

Jay did take a breath, but his frustration still seemed to bubble inside him.

"Let me taste 'em," Dre said, looking over Jayden's newest failure. Dre took a bite. "They actually aren't that bad. Just missing something."

"Like what?" Jay asked.

"I don't know, Jay. You got to figure that part out. But look, try these. I brought them like you told me to do in your weirdo note." Dre handed Jay a large cookie.

"Note? What are you talking—dude!" said Jay. "These are so good, Dre."

"They're my recipe. But it took me, like, eight tries to get it right."

"You lying," said Jayden with a laugh. "Eight tries? The Great Dre—yeah, right!"

"No lies here. I messed up every time, until I got it right," he said, taking a bite of one of his own cookies. "I call them PB and Dre Drop Cookies."

"They are really good. You're going to win the competition for sure."

"Maybe. But come look at this, Jay," Dre said. "I figured out this trick when I was messing up all those times. You know when you always get egg-shells in your batter—well, check this," DeAndre said, showing Jayden how to hold his hand. "You see that? Clean crack each time and no shell."

"That was awesome. I'm going to try that."

"Since I'm here, I want to try making my pastry. I've been working on this recipe. I haven't got it quite right, yet." DeAndre pulled out folded paper from his pocket. "Here it is."

"You write down your recipes?" asked Jayden.

"For sure. My grandma always says: 'How else are you going to remember what you did last time when you are making your own flavor?' Ever since she told me that, I've been writing my recipes down. It's really helped build my confidence in the kitchen."

Clyde's ears perked up at that word: *confidence*. He felt like he didn't know what the word meant, but he knew what it was in his heart.

Confidence.

DeAndre flattened the sheet, and the boys looked it over.

"Is that going to be your second entry?" asked Jayden.

"Yep. If I can get it just right."

For the next few hours, the boys baked together, giving each other tips and trying out new things. Jayden jotted down ingredients he added, and which ones worked best. DeAndre worked and reworked his pastry dough until it was the consistency he liked.

Finally, each boy's creation was finished, baked, and pulled out to cool.

"Moment of truth, right?" said Jay as he handed DeAndre his cookie.

"Let's go," said Dre as he plated a pastry for Jay.

Both boys dug in.

"Mmmmmm," they both responded.

"This pastry is the best I've tasted," said Jay.

"Yeah, I guess it turned out pretty good. Not perfect, but pretty good," said Dre. "And your cookie, you figured out the missing thing. What did you do differently?"

"I crushed up some of Auntie's peppermint candies—a cup, to be exact," said Jayden, pointing at his newly written recipe. "And I added a few more things, like white chocolate chips, some nutmeg, and a secret ingredient, which I'm not telling." Jayden laughed. "But they still aren't where I want them to be. I'm gonna try again."

"Cool," said Dre, cleaning up his things and heading for the door. "Catch you tomorrow, Jay."

"Peace, Dre."

A calm came over the kitchen. Jayden moved through his recipe once more, writing down changes as he went.

"Bringing in DeAndre was brilliant, Clyde," said Rosie as they watched Jayden plate his last batch. "He actually seemed to like doing it this time."

"Yeah, this plan seemed to give him what he needed—what did Dre call it?" said Barkley.

"Confidence," answered Noodles.

"Do you know what that is?" asked Clyde.

She did know that word. "It means believing in yourself, in what you are able to do," answered Noodles.

"Just like Clyde, when he's in the kitchen," added

Barkley. "Even when you mess up, you still believe in yourself."

"Yeah," said Clyde. "Confidence."

Just then, Jayden walked over to Auntie's recipe book and pulled it out. He thumbed through until he found what he was looking for: a bright pink paper with Auntie's handwriting on it.

"Second dessert of my choice," Jayden said to himself. "Auntie's new meringue."

"Wait, wasn't that the one he ruined the last time he tried it?" asked Barkley.

"Yeah, when he decided to drop out the first time?" said Noodles.

Uh-oh. Was it possible to become *too* confident?

Chapter 11
The Sweet Taste
of Victory

Starting with Monday, the next couple of days were all the same.

Jayden would wake up. He'd meet DeAndre and the two would take the bus to summer camp.

Then they'd come back at the end of the day and hit the kitchen, both working like mad scientists in a tasty-smelling laboratory. Mixing and stirring and failing—but trying again and again.

Each day, Jayden got closer and closer to Friday: the day the summer camp judges would decide who would be competing on Saturday.

On Thursday evening, Jayden called to Auntie and Durrell, "I think they are ready!"

"These cookies are even better than before," said Durrell, sinking his teeth into the chocolatey and pepperminty morsels.

"Is this my meringue recipe?" said Auntie with a smile.

"It started off that way," said Jayden, "but I added in my own flavor."

"That's what I like to hear," said Auntie. She took a big bite. "This is divine, Jay. You should be so proud!"

The smile on his face told the pups that he certainly was.

The pups waited all day Friday for Jayden and DeAndre to come home. Had Jayden made it to the next round?

"There's the bus," called Barkley.

Jayden flew off the bus calling, "Auntie! Auntie!" His voice bounced off the street and apartment walls.

Auntie opened the door, and Jayden ran right into

her open arms. "I made it, Auntie. Both me and Dre. We'll be competing in the bakeoff tomorrow for five hundred dollars."

"This calls for a celebration," said Auntie, and she and Jayden headed inside.

"Welp, I guess we did it," said Barkley. "Jayden made it to the final round: the actual bakeoff." Technically, their mission was complete.

"No way," said Clyde. "We've got to keep with him to the very end of this mission. We only got him through the first round. We can't give up on him now."

Clyde hoped that they'd given Jayden enough practice and ideas to help him come up with a win.

* * *

The next morning, people piled into a large indoor stadium-like place that had seats lined from the wooden floor all the way up—almost to the ceiling! On the stadium floor, there were a bunch of tables and ovens and materials and ingredients. Even an envelope that held the mystery recipe that the young bakers would have to make for the first time. Everything they would need was right there within reach.

The pups hid out of view near the stadium floor but underneath some of the bleachers.

"Twenty-five," whispered Clyde to the rest of his team.

"Huh?" said Rosie.

"Twenty-five tables and ovens. Which means twenty-five in the whole competition."

"That's a lot of young bakers to beat," said Barkley.

"But Jayden can do it! I just know he can," said Clyde. The familiar swirling feeling returned to his tummy, tying his insides into knot after knot.

"There he is," whispered Noodles. DeAndre and Jayden entered the arena. Each looked at a small sheet of paper with a number written on it.

"Eight," said Jayden.

"Fifteen," said DeAndre. They gave each other good-luck handshakes and went to the table labeled with their numbers.

Jayden looked up at the bleachers. More and more people were filing into the seats. He gulped.

"JAY!" he heard voices yell. He turned and saw Auntie and Durrell, but not just them—his whole family had shown up. Granddad and his aunts, uncles, and cousins, too. They screamed for him from their high-up seats.

"You got this, Jay!" Durrell's voice boomed.

Jayden began preparing his station. He pulled out labels and permanent markers. He labeled each of the ingredients, including the measuring cups.

The puppies watched with tails wiggling with glee.

"That's all you, Clydie," said Rosie, patting him on the cheek.

The emcee got onto the microphone and welcomed everyone. Then he started the timer and the young bakers were off.

In the time allotted, Jayden would have to make the two treats he had entered into the competition, but he also had to make the challenging mystery one: a Toffee Pretzel Bar.

Noodles's nose glared brightly. "He's definitely feeling nervous," she said.

"And he's off to a bumpy start," said Clyde. The pups gasped as Jayden dropped two eggs on the floor, spilled some flour, and misplaced his whisk. When he started on the pretzel bar recipe, he seemed to freeze, looking over it as if it were written in a language he couldn't read and didn't understand.

Jayden balled up his fists. But then he took a deep breath and relaxed his fingers.

"Look at DeAndre go," said Noodles. Over at Station 15, DeAndre moved through the kitchen with ease, whipping and mixing and flowing. For a moment, Jayden and DeAndre caught each other's eyes. Both boys flashed the other a thumbs-up and returned to their creations.

For the rest of the competition, Jayden pushed through until the end.

But Clyde's tummy flipped and twirled and somersaulted.

All the bakers plated their treats and stood back,

watching as the judges visited each station. Shortly after, they approached the emcee who then moved to the microphone.

At that moment, Clyde doubled over, holding his tummy tight and whimpering.

"Clydie, are you all right?!" asked Rosie. All the pups huddled around him, stroking him gently.

"Deep breaths, Pup. Deep breaths," whispered Rosie.

"And now for the winners," said the emcee. "In third place, Jayden Wright with his Fly Choco-Peppermint Cookies, Auntie's Meringue, and a well-executed Toffee Pretzel Bar."

The crowd erupted and Jayden smiled as he approached the stage.

The emcee went on to announce the second-place winner—a tall girl with dark black hair and pale skin.

Finally, the emcee began again: "And the first-prize winner of the five hundred dollars is— DeAndre Robinson with his PB and Dre Drop Cookies, his Dark and Ruby Chocolate–filled pastry, and a perfect Toffee Pretzel Bar."

Jayden leapt up and down. He and DeAndre high-fived right there on the stage.

"You rocked it, Dre," said Jayden.

"You too," he answered.

"Five hundred dollars—oh man!"

Back under the bleachers, the pups patted Clyde.

"Did you hear that, Clydie?" said Rosie with worry in her voice. "Jayden got third place."

"He did," whispered Clyde.

"He did."

"Woo-hoo!" shouted Clyde, who vaulted up into a flying flip right there under the bleachers.

"Clydie—you're okay!" cried Rosie.

"Clyde, your tummy!" yelled Noodles.

"Your tongue," called Barkley.

"Can you taste that?" answered Clyde. He stuck out his tongue as if tasting the air.

No longer did Clyde's tummy twist and turn. Instead, both his tongue and belly glowed brightly as he hovered in the air.

"Mmmm, vanilla and maple cupcakes," Clyde said turning his head one way. "Peppermint cookies, toffee bars," he continued, turning this way and that, "carrot-date-almond cake."

"You can taste all those things just by sticking your tongue out?" asked Noodles.

"I can?" said Clyde, realizing it for the first time himself. "I can!"

"Clydie, your new talent is born!"

"A new talent tied to my tummy and taste buds— that's *my* kind of talent," said Clyde. "And third place for Jayden, plus first for DeAndre. That's pup-tastic!"

Boy, did victory taste sweet!

Chapter 12
Mission Complete and
a Cherry on Top

"What a mission," said Rosie as the pups sat at

the countertop watching Clyde work his magic

in the kitchen.

"I'll say," said Noodles. "Failures and triumphs. And boosts of confidence."

Clyde flew through the air singing "Nachos, nachos, yeah," to himself. After this mission, he had a great idea of what to add to his Na-cho Grandpup's Nachos to make them even better—though, nobody had a chance to try them out the last time.

"It's not always easy learning a new skill," said Barkley, "especially if it's something that doesn't come naturally to you."

"Yep, like learning how to make the perfect cookies!" said Rosie. "But this mission definitely showed me that you'll make mistakes as you learn— and that's okay."

"That's actually how you learn in the first place!" added Noodles.

"And you also have to practice and believe in yourself, right, Clyde?" said Barkley.

"Egg-xactly," said Clyde. "Confidence! With practice and believing in yourself, your skills will grow. That's the true recipe for success!"

Clyde placed all the plates of his nacho dish in front of his team. Each pup chowed down, barely taking any breaths.

But as they ate, Clyde sat up for a moment and said, "I wonder how Jayden is doing?"

"Well, let's find out," responded Rosie. The heart on her chest began to glow. Jayden's kitchen appeared in the heart. And soon, Jayden, too, as he stood at the counter, focusing closely on a cake he was icing.

Jayden placed three cherries in the very center of the cake. Then he piped a flower onto the cake, making a scrunched-up face. He picked up a cake tool and scooped the flower off, using the tool then to smooth the icing down. Jayden began again, piping the flower another time.

"Perfect," he said after finishing the iced flower and stepping back to admire his work. Jayden carefully lifted the cake and took it into the living room. As he entered, everyone sitting in the room began singing: "Happy birthday to you!"

Jayden carried the cake right over to Auntie, who beamed.

"Look how beautiful that is," said a different aunt. "You made this all by yourself?"

"I did," said Jayden. "Even made the recipe up on my own."

"Well, you outdid yourself today, Jay," said Granddad.

Jayden smiled. "It only took me ten tries to get it right. But I got it!"

"Sounds about right," said Auntie with a wink.

Rosie's heart dimmed.

"Did you see his piping? It was pup-tastic. Not even I am *that* good at icing a cake," said Clyde.

"I'd call that beautiful cake a success. Too bad I'm not actually there to taste it."

"Jayden really grew and accomplished so much: Making it to the bakeoff, taking third place, continuing to practice his skills," said Rosie.

"I think we can say this mission was definitely a success, too," added Noodles. "One of our best!"

"Even we are getting better at what *we* do—" said Rosie.

"Even when it's hard," added Barkley.

"Being able to grow and improve and feel good about what we can do is magic at its best!" said Rosie.

Each pup crunched in agreement.

Read all of the Love Puppies' paw-some adventures!

■SCHOLASTIC
scholastic.com

LOVEPUPPIES